Disney
Beauty and the Beast

Illustrated by Jaime Diaz Studios
Illustration script developed by Christina Wilsdon
Lettering by Kelly Hume

Published by
Louis Weber, C.E.O.
Publications International, Ltd.
7373 North Cicero Avenue
Lincolnwood, Illinois 60712

Ground Floor, 59 Gloucester Place
London W1U 8JJ

Customer Service: 1-800-595-8484 or customer_service@pilbooks.com

www.pilbooks.com

p i kids is a registered trademark of Publications International, Ltd.
Look and Find is a registered trademark of Publications International, Ltd.,
in the United States and in Canada.

8 7 6 5 4 3 2 1

Manufactured in China.

ISBN-10: 1-60553-316-5
ISBN-13: 978-1-60553-316-2

pi kids® publications international, ltd.

Noemi's book

Once upon a time, there was a kind and beautiful girl named Belle who taught an enchanted Beast how to love and earn the love of others.

Take a look at the world of Beauty and the Beast. It is full of adventure and romance. Can you find these characters from this wonderful story?

Belle

The Beast

Gaston

Maurice

Lumiere

Cogsworth

Mrs. Potts

The signs read: OPEN, CLOSED, THIS END UP

It's a hustle-bustle morning in the village and Belle is off to visit the bookstore — again. She's a girl who loves to read, but Gaston doesn't mind. He plans to marry her whether she wants him or not!

Can you find Belle and Gaston? Can you find these other people in the village, too?

Belle

Le Fou

Gaston

The butcher

The chimney sweep

The baker

The triplets

The bookseller

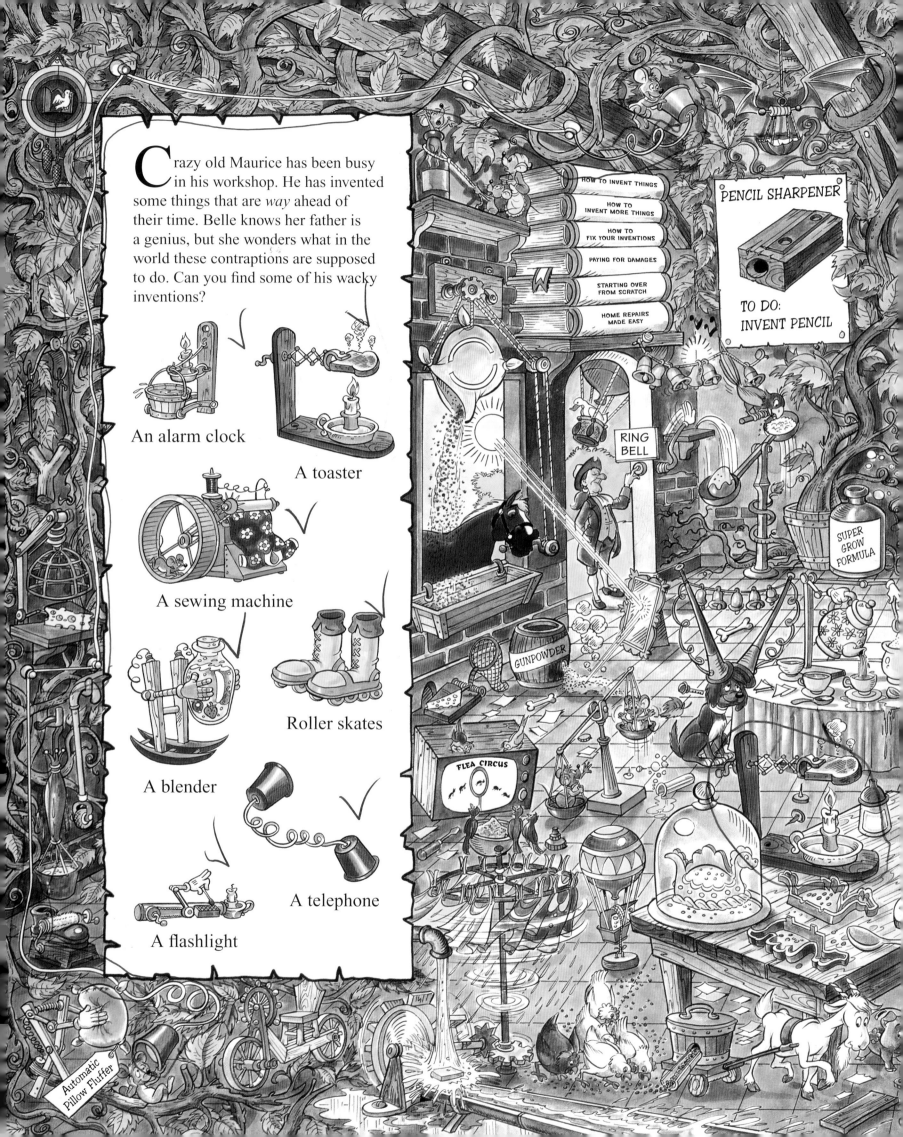

Crazy old Maurice has been busy in his workshop. He has invented some things that are *way* ahead of their time. Belle knows her father is a genius, but she wonders what in the world these contraptions are supposed to do. Can you find some of his wacky inventions?

An alarm clock

A toaster

A sewing machine

A blender

Roller skates

A telephone

A flashlight

HOW TO INVENT THINGS

HOW TO INVENT MORE THINGS

HOW TO FIX YOUR INVENTIONS

PAYING FOR DAMAGES

STARTING OVER FROM SCRATCH

HOME REPAIRS MADE EASY

PENCIL SHARPENER

TO DO: INVENT PENCIL

RING BELL

SUPER GROW FORMULA

GUNPOWDER

FLEA CIRCUS

Automatic Pillow Fluffer

Gaston hoped his marriage proposal would make a splash, but this isn't exactly what he had in mind! As for Belle, she thinks Gaston is all washed up.

Take a look around Belle's little farm. Can you find these ladies who *do* have eyes for Gaston?

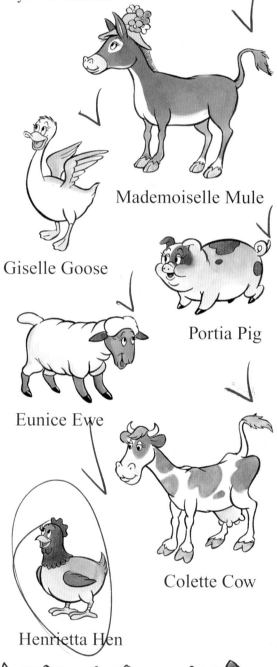

Mademoiselle Mule

Giselle Goose

Portia Pig

Eunice Ewe

Colette Cow

Henrietta Hen

HUMPTY DUMPTY WAS PUSHED!

The Beast has everything his heart desires … almost. If only he had someone to love who would love him back and break the spell. Until the day she arrives, the Beast's only companions are his enchanted servants.

Can you find these members of the Beast's household?

Lumiere

Cogsworth

Mrs. Potts

Coatrack

Chip

Footstool

Featherduster

HOW TO MAKE FRIENDS

HOW TO MEET GIRLS

Gaston thinks he's a fine specimen of a man—and when he brags, people listen! Don't plug *your* ears, either, if you know what's good for you.

Any minute now, Gaston will notice that he's missing a few things. Can you find them?

His foolish friend ✓

His mirror ✓

A letter from his mother ✓

His quiver ✓

His blunderbuss

His comb ✓

A picture of his favorite person ✓

Belle doesn't have much of an appetite tonight, but Mrs. Potts and Lumiere are sure they can tempt her to try just a tiny bit of something. Perhaps a little music will help.

Can you find these tempting morsels that the kitchen has whipped up for Belle's first supper in the castle?

Caesar salad

Aged cheese

Angel food cake

French bread

Chilled asparagus

Chicken a la king

Atten-*shun!* Gaston's angry mob is sure the Beast is a terrible monster. Now everyone in the castle, from the lowliest dustbin to the fanciest featherduster, must report for duty to protect the Beast and his home.

Look for these soldiers as they battle the villagers.

General Junque

Private Pillowfight

Sergeant Snipp

Lieutenant Ladle

Brigadier Buckethead

Corporal Cookpot

Admiral Armor

The Beast was not the only enchanted person living in the magical castle. When Belle helped turn him back into a prince, the enchanted objects turned back into their real selves, too.

Can you find these members of the Beast's household who are feeling like themselves again?

Cogsworth

Lumiere

Footstool

Mrs. Potts

Chip

Featherduster

Wardrobe

Take a closer look at the world of Belle and the Beast. Can you find these characters, too?

- Phillipe
- Le Fou
- Chip
- The pretty triplets
- Featherduster
- Footstool

Go back to Belle's village to find these characters with noses in books.

- A cat reading *Puss in Boots*
- A girl reading *Cinderella*
- A cook reading a cookbook
- A nursemaid reading *Mother Goose*
- A boy reading a diary
- A frog reading *The Frog Prince*